Lydia's 12 Christmases

Emunah Short Stories

Janice Wee

Published by Janice Wee, 2024.

LYDIA'S 12 CHRISTMASES

First edition. December 1, 2024.

Copyright © 2024 Janice Wee.

ISBN: 979-8230251316

Written by Janice Wee.

Also by Janice Wee

Max the Cat
The Scouts
Escape To Long Hill
Max & Friends

Tales From Singapore
Singapore's Runaway
Two Worlds, One Love & a Serial Killer
Two Worlds
Naughty Little Nonya
Little Nonya's Escapades

Standalone
Escape
Sweetcorn Suzie

Watch for more at www.janicewee.com.

This year, it wasn't a white Christmas, but a red one — blood red.

One - Denver : Christmas Baby

Lydia hated Christmas. It clashed with her birthday.

It was five past eleven, the night before Christmas. Fairy lights and glowing candles lit the hall, as Christmas carols played in the background.

The kids were with engaged in party games; Denver's pregnant wife, Sally, snuggled under his arm. He felt her hard round belly. Their unborn child was moving to the music's tempo, enjoying the party as much as they did.

"Honey," Sally paled. "I think my water bag burst."

Buzzing with joy Denver held her hand. "It's a month too soon. Are you sure?"

"I'm like, ninety percent positive that baby wants to come out now," she bit her lip, her fingers trembled.

"She's an impatient one," Denver kissed her cheek.

Turning to Fred, he announced. "Baby's on the way."

"Go," his buddy and party host, waved them off. "Your boys can stay over with us tonight."

Denver drove off, with Sally in the passenger seat. The nearest hospital was a full two hour's drive away. Enough time to get her to the delivery room.

Sally face contorted with pain as she held her precious belly.

Denver recognised the signs from Sally's past pregnancies.

Labour had begun.

Bang!

"Oh no." Denver's face turned ice-cold. "Not now!"

"What happened?" Sally panted, her face drained from colour as she clenched her teeth. Another wave of labour pain, from what he had read.

"We blew a tyre," Denver pulled his hair. A bad habit he couldn't kick when stressed.

There was no time to waste. They had to hitch a ride or get a cab.

There's a bench on the sidewalk where she could rest while he got help.

"I'll hitch a ride or hail a cab," he helped her settle on the bench.

Cars whizzed past without stopping. More than a few cabs drove by, but all were occupied.

An empty cab approached with a green vacant sign.

His heart leaped with anticipation.

The driver locked eyes with him, then looked away. The green vacant signed turned an occupied red, dashing Denver's hopes.

"Stop," Denver chased after the empty cab like a dog chasing after cars. "Please," he pleaded as the cab disappeared into the horizon.

It's Christmas Eve.

Where is the Christmas Spirit?

Is Christmas nothing more than a season of self indulgent partying?

Denver couldn't help ruminating.

"Sir," an officer grabbed his arm. "You are under arrest for disturbing the peace."

"Officer," Denver stared at the policeman in disbelief. "My wife is in labour."

"That's what they all say," the officer reached for his handcuffs.

"Stop!" Sally hugged her belly and hobbled over. "My husband and I need to get to the hospital before my baby pops out."

She bent over, and hugged her belly. A pained moan escaped her lips. It broke Denver's heart to see his wife in such agony.

"Please help us," she cried. "My baby is coming."

The officer shrugged. With an awkward glance, he released Denver. "You may go now."

"I have to get to the hospital. Can you get us a ride?" Sally begged the policeman.

He turned around and looked at his own vehicle - a motorcycle. "I don't think that would work."

Denver closed his eyes.

"God, if you are real, please help us get a ride."

When he opened his eyes, a taxi pulled over right in front of him.

A Christmas Miracle!

"Thanks anyway, Officer," Denver nodded at the police.

"Dear, our ride's waiting," he grinned as he helped Sally into the taxi.

Sally was tense throughout the ride. She seemed to be in agony. He rubbed soothing circles on her back, trying to help her to relax and to ease the pain.

Tears streamed down her cheeks. "Make it stop," she whispered as the cab stopped at the hospital's taxi stand.

"Dear, we are here," he whispered with all the tenderness in his heart. Carefully, he scooped his wife in his arms and carried her into the hospital.

"Hurry, she is in labour," he told the staff. They put her in a wheelchair and wheeled her into the delivery ward.

By then, Sally was in her own world. A world Denver knew swirled with excruciating torment. From what she'd told him, he wondered at the strength of all mothers who survived the ordeal.

"Don't push yet," the midwife reminded Sally. "You're not fully dilated."

"Breathe dear," Denver reminded his wife as he massaged her back.

The dulcet notes of the classic Christmas carol filled the room.

$$\times$$

SILENT NIGHT, HOLY Night.

Huff, huff,

All is

SCREAM!

Calm,

Sally released the urge to push by screaming her lungs out.

Huff, huff, SCREAM!

By breathing, he didn't mean for her to scream.

Okay, she screamed when she was delivering Oliver.

She screamed just as much while in labour with Aaron.

That was the only way she could stop herself from pushing before the baby's ready to come out, or so she explained.

Whatever her reason, Denver couldn't stand it anymore.

"Doctor, please help my wife," Denver panicked. It was not their first child. Or even their second.

Yet Denver was freaked out as when their eldest, Oliver was born.

Huff, huff, SCREAM!

"An epidural will ease the pain," the doctor told him.

"Do it," he replied, forgetting his wife's terror of needles.

Big mistake.

That look of horror on her face when she saw the needle made him regret his impulsive decision.

"Relax. I'll inject your spine and you won't feel anything," the doctor, tried to calm Sally.

"No!" She screamed, protesting with a good hard kick that missed the doctor by less than an inch.

Stunned, he dropped the syringe.

$$\times$$

HUFF, HUFF, SCREAM!

Another nurse approached her with a fresh syringe, only to receive a good hard kick from the flailing woman.

"I'm sorry," the medical staff told Denver. "It's too dangerous to give her the epidural."

Yeah.

It's too dangerous for *them* to come near her with that needle.

"Here, breathe this. It will take the edge off the pain," the midwife gave her a mouthpiece.

Sally refused to breathe in the laughing gas. Instead she used the equipment the way she always did.

Huff, huff, SCREAM!

She screamed into the muzzle, using it to muffle her cries. That was considerate of her, though it meant she wasn't using anything to ease the pain.

A doctor, needle-free, examined Sally.

"She's fully dilated," he announced.

"You may push now," the midwife encouraged.

"Go for it," Denver whispered into his wife's ear.

Sally strained in effort, pushing in place of the screams. Her face contorted, as if she was trying to shit out a watermelon.

Finally, the baby's head popped out, large, curious eyes taking in her surroundings before she was fully in this world. She had a head of pale curly hair. The adorable babe stared at him as she gurgled.

Denver's heart welled up with love for his almost-born baby girl. They knew her gender ahead of time through the scans; a pink crib and cupboard of pretty dresses awaited their new daughter in the baby's room.

"One last push," the midwife urged Sally.

Sally strained, pushing with everything she had.

The rest of the baby's body slid out.

Though her body's sore and exhausted, the pain's gone.

Sally's terrified of the sight of blood. It didn't surprise Denver when she shut her eyes, refusing to look until the blood had been cleaned away.

Denver chuckled at his Paradoxically Phobic wife. For a woman brave enough to give birth without pain relief, she was a coward when it came to needles and blood.

"Would you like to hold your baby?" The midwife offered the curious bundle swaddled in pink blankets to Sally and Denver.

Sally radiated joy and motherly pride when she accepted the bundle. Cradling the baby in her arms, she seemed to have forgotten the ordeal she had just gone through. "Little Lydia," she laughed as she gazed into their baby's adoring eyes.

"Happy Birthday Lydia," Denver cooed as he kissed their tiny daughter's forehead. "And Merry Christmas!"

Two - Oliver : Angelic Gremlins

"Mummy, I don't want to wear this," Lydia pouted, tugging at the neckline of her pristine, white lace dress. "It's so itchy!"

"Itchy itchy, scratchy scratchy, up and down my, back," Aaron sang-song teased Lydia, earning a smack on his head in return.

"No fair," she pointed at her brothers. "They don't have to wear scratchy, uncomfortable dresses. Why must I?"

"We have to wear these stupid bow ties," Oliver tugged at the crimson bow that was tied around his neck. He could empathise with convicts on the death row, sentenced to the noose.

"Can't we wear t-shirts and shorts?" Lydia squirmed. "My Elmo t-shirt and red shorts are the best!"

"There's a dress code for carollers," Dad tweaked Lydia's nose. "If you want to join the group, you have to follow the rules."

"Rules, spules," whined Lydia, the baby of the family..

"There's no such word as 'spules'," Aaron corrected her.

"Yes, there is," Lydia protested.

"No there isn't," Oliver snapped back. "You made it up."

"I made that word, so it's a new word now." Thinks-she-knows-it-all Lydia gave her brothers that annoying smug look which for some unknown reason, won the adults over.

"Come on, kids, or we'll be late," Daddy herded the trio towards the door.

"How about our confetti?" Aaron ran back in, rummaging through the mess known as the boys' room.

"I've got it," Oliver pulled out a large bag of hole punch confetti, painstakingly collected from all the aunties and uncles who worked in offices. Every year, from June onwards, he'd sweet talk every contact he had into collecting dots from all the hole punchers in their office which he'd keep in a large bag for the annual confetti battles. He'd run errands in return for six months worth of paper chad.

For six years, he could keep the entire bag for himself but when Aaron turned seven a year ago, he had to give some of his confetti to his brother. Now with Lydia joining the carollers, he had to collect enough ammo for all three of them.

"All mine," little Lydia made a grab for the bag, but Oliver held it just out of her reach.

"I collected it, so it's mine," he stated.

"Ollie," Mummy handed him two empty paper bags. "Share with your brother and sister."

"I know," Oliver sighed. He'd expected that. "I'll split it in the car."

As Daddy drove the family to church, Oliver admired the scenery. The houses, trees and lamp posts on both sides of the street were decked out in Christmas lights, stars, bells, angels and festive decor.

"Joy to the World," Mum sang in her soprano voice.

"The Lord is come," Daddy joined in with his deep baritone.

While Oliver carefully poured some of his precious confetti into smaller bags for Aaron and Lydia, his siblings joined their parents as they sang their way to church.

"Why is my confetti bag so small?" Lydia pouted.

"Because you are the smallest," Aaron chuckled.

"How come you have more than us?" Lydia jabbed Oliver with her finger.

"Because I'm the one who worked for it." It irked Oliver that he had to part with half his ammo. They should be grateful to get any, since they didn't have to lift a finger for their confetti.

"I give you mine, and you give me yours," Lydia handed her little bag to Oliver as she eyed his loot.

"No," Oliver, hugged his bag. "I'm going to need this."

"Why?" Lydia asked.

"Because Bryan will want his revenge. I need to defend myself," Oliver replied.

"I will protect you," tiny Lydia flexed her scrawny arm. "I will beat up anyone who tries to bully my big brother."

"Thanks sis," Oliver side-hugged little Lydia.

"But I'm not swapping bags with you."

They arrived at the church gates. Distracted, Lydia waved at her friends.

"Meet us at the Candlelight Service," said Daddy as he dropped them off.

"And Oliver," Mummy called out. "Take care of Aaron and Lydia."

"I'm big enough to take care of myself," Lydia protested as the car drove off.

Brimming with excitement, Lydia ran off the join the other girls.

An old man wearing dark shades, carried an accordion gig bag while he tapped the ground with a white cane. Uncle Lionel looked like he could use some help. The old musician played the accordion for Sunday School.

"Need a hand with that?" Oliver walked up to the musician.

"Yes," the old man looked tired, heaving that hefty accordion bag around.

Oliver carried the accordion case while Aaron chatted with Uncle Lionel as they made their way up the bus.

Oliver's baby sister boarded the bus with her friends, the tinselled halo on her head, playing the part of an angelic cherub to perfection. It tickled him to watch his vocal and headstrong gremlin-of-a-sister, sitting so demure and obedient, listening intently to carol leader's instructions.

"No confetti until 10pm," the senior announced.

Lydia nodded, her eyes wide and ridiculously innocent as she gripped onto her purse which held her share of confetti.

"Sequence 1," the carol leader declared as the troop formed a line outside the gate of the house.

Uncle Lionel sat on his stool, playing the accordion as the carollers marched past him singing the opening carol, "O Come, All Ye Faithful."

After a medley of carols, at the carol leader's signal, the room fell silent.

The narrator's crystal clear voice, cut through the lull. "For unto us a child is born, unto us a son is given: and the government shall be upon his shoulder: and his name shall be called Wonderful, Counseller, The mighty God, The everlasting Father, The Prince of Peace."

The performers sang the next three songs a cappella, in four part harmony. Oliver and Aaron, whose voices had yet to break, sang the tenor portion while little Lydia sang alto with her friends.

Their performance complete, the hosts invited the carollers to the dining room where refreshments had been prepared for them.

"I thought they have turkey," Lydia whined. "Aaron said last year, he had roast beef, turkey and pizza. Why only sandwiches?" For a tiny girl, her voice was embarrassingly loud.

"Lower your voice. People can hear." Flustered, Oliver hushed the pampered princess.

"We got turkey and roast beef and pizza in the last few houses before going back to church," Aaron bit into his sandwich. "Don't know why you complain. These are good."

"I don't like cold sandwiches," Lydia pouted as she reached for a cup of grape juice.

"Anyway," Aaron waved his arms haphazardly, accidentally knocking Lydia's cup, spilling the purple liquid on Lydia's white dress.

"No!" Lydia screamed. "You spoiled my new dress."

"You can wash it off when we get home," Aaron shrugged.

"You did it on purpose so I get kicked out of the bus," she pulled Aaron's hair.

"Let go!" Aaron hit her back. "I did not."

"You just hit me on purpose," Lydia kicked her brother.

"You pulled my hair," Aaron pushed her away.

Sighing, Oliver walked up to his younger siblings to break up the fight. "Aaron, Lydia, apologise to each other now or I will tell Daddy and Mummy. Then they will never let you go carolling again," he glared at squabbling siblings.

"Sorry," Aaron and Lydia chorused. From their glares, he doubted they meant it.

Teacher Elisa knelt before Lydia and blotted the liquid with a clean cloth. "Come with me," she cooed. "We'll wash it off."

"Are you going to kick me out because my white dress turned purple," Lydia was so distraught, Oliver felt sorry for his pesky little sister.

"Of course not," the teacher laughed. We'll get the juice off your dress now, then we can go to the next house.

The carollers brought Christmas cheer from one house to another, filling their bulging bellies with food and drink. Then came the moment they had all been waiting for.

"It's ten now. Confetti!" The carol leader threw confetti at his fellow senior, launching the confetti fight in the middle of the bus.

Squeals and screams filled the air as the carollers tossed confetti at one another. Oliver had a bagful of dots poured on his head, courtesy of his nemesis, Bryan. Undaunted, he shook the confetti off his hair and body, collecting it into the bag, to reuse on the next victim.

"Hey!" Aaron screamed as Lydia threw confetti at his face. "You threw it in my eye! It hurts!"

"Time out!" The carol leader hollered to the disappointed moans of the fellow singers. The senior brought a flask to Aaron. He poured a cup of warm water and used it to flush the confetti out of Aaron's tearing eye.

"I'm sorry," Lydia whispered. Contrite.

As punishment, the carol leader confiscated the rest of Lydia's confetti. "This is to stop you from blinding any of us."

The group behaved like angels in each house, but gremlins on the bus. Lydia ate her fill roast turkey and roast beef, stuffing herself until Oliver worried she'd burst the seams of her dress. The carollers saved their biggest performance for the final home of the night.

The carol leader and narrator played the parts of Joseph and Mary in the re-enactment of the manger scene as they performed in that final house - a mansion overflowing with onlookers. The carollers ended the performance with the song, "Christmas isn't Christmas, till it happens, in your heart."

The ride back to church was somber as the carollers reflected on the message they shared in that last home.

Aaron, seated beside Oliver asked, "What does that mean Christmas in your heart?"

"Christmas isn't about fun and parties," Oliver explained. "Two thousand years ago, God came down on earth in the form of baby Jesus."

"Why would he do that?" Aaron asked.

"Because everyone has sinned - said or done or thought bad things in their lives," Oliver replied. "God is holy and just. All sins must be punished and the punishment of sin is death."

"That's harsh," Aaron shuddered. "Who hasn't even thought of bad things before?"

"Instead of punishing us, God loved us so much he became a man, Jesus Christ, who died on the cross to pay for our sins, in our place," Oliver explained.

"Jesus paid for your forgiveness with his blood on that cross two thousand years ago."

"So what do we do to be forgiven?" Aaron asked.

"Acknowledge that you are a sinner and believe that Jesus died on the cross to pay for your sins. Accept the forgiveness he bought for you and trust Jesus as your Lord and Saviour," Oliver replied.

"How?" Aaron asked.

"Pray with me," Oliver said as he closed his eyes and bowed his head in prayer. "Dear God, I am a sinner. I'm sorry. Thank you, Jesus for dying on the cross to pay for my sins. Be my Lord and Saviour. In Jesus name I pray amen."

They soon arrived at the church. Aaron looked radiant with newfound joy as they headed to the sanctuary with Lydia to find Dad and Mum.

Service was surreal. Towards the end, the pastor lit his candle and used it to light the worship leader's candle. The overhead lights went off. Then each candle lit another until everyone held a flickering light.

The clock struck twelve.

The congregation chorused, "Merry Christmas!"

People in front, turned around to shake their hands, exchanging Christmas greetings.

Lydia sagged.

Looking up at Oliver, her eyes brimming with tears, she asked.

"How come everyone says Merry Christmas but no one wished me Happy Birthday?"

Three - Abigail : Sweet Sixteen

"I hate Christmas," Lydia scowled as she slammed the phone.

"What happened?" Abigail asked the birthday girl.

"Joey said he'd come, but had to back out last minute because his grandma wouldn't let him skip their family Christmas party." Lydia slumped forward. Her eyes glistened with unshed tears. The girl had a crush on Joey since she was twelve; she'd turn beetroot-red when he talked to her in church, but the moron was totally oblivious to her feelings for him.

"Hey, I'm here," Abigail gave her old pal a big bear hug. "Troy's coming and he's way hotter than Joey."

"Joey's nicer," Lydia shrugged, staring into the distance, a wistful look in her eyes, her lips in a soft, gentle curve. "Troy's too stuck up, like he's too good for everyone else."

"If he thought he's too good for the rest of us, then why is he coming?" Abigail pointed out.

"I don't know. Maybe mister too-sexy-for-my-friends pities us ordinary folks?" Lydia's laugh sounded forced. Abigail suspected Lydia had a mild crush on Troy as well, but refused to acknowledge it, thinking he's out of her league. She'd observed their interactions and believed that Troy fancied Lydia too.

"Enough talk about me," Lydia's eyes twinkled with mischief. "How about you? What do you think of my brother Aaron?"

"What about Aaron?" Abigail didn't like where the conversation was heading.

"You two are so close, I smell love in the air." Lydia teased. Abigail couldn't stand that smug, annoying look as if Lydia knew everything.

"There's nothing going on between Aaron and I," Abigail's cheeks felt stupidly hot. "We're best friends!"

"Friends-to-lovers is a popular trope," Lydia wagged her hand.

"This is real life, not some story book," Abigail twirled her hair - a nervous habit she couldn't break.

"Lydia, your guests are here," Aaron poked his head into Lydia's room.

"Hi Abby" he waved a rolled up comic book when he noticed Abigail, "I got the latest issue."

"Coming," Lydia headed out to receive her guests - a mix of school mates and church friends. Each arrived with a birthday gift which they gave to Lydia and a Christmas gift for the gift exchange which went under the Christmas tree. It was a Sweet Sixteen Birthday and Christmas Party.

Oliver and Aaron had laboured all day to set up an archway at the entrance with twinkling fairy lights and snowflakes, with a sign "Merry Birthday Lydia!" Framed in green garlands, red berries and sugar pink bows.

A towering Christmas tree decked out with butterflies and unicorns, lit with red and green string lights added to the atmosphere.

A table on one side of the room was laden with roast turkey, roast beef, pizza and doughnuts. Aunt Sally, who was an amazing chef, cooked all of it with Uncle Denver's help.

Abigail cringed at envy's sting. Lydia had no idea how lucky, how well-loved she was.

The center of the room had been cleared for party games and to use as a dance floor.

The games began.

Troy lost.

The penalty?

By popular demand - the loser kisses the Birthday girl.

"What?" Lydia looked horrified.

"It's in good fun," Abigail teased.

"How would you like it if Aaron had to kiss you?" Lydia retorted.

"Well, he doesn't," Abigail laughed as she led Lydia to the center of the dance floor.

"Let's get it over with," Troy blushed as he brushed her hair off her face. "I don't bite."

"Alright," Lydia chuckled, her cheeks bright pink. "How bad can it be?"

As the group cheered, their lips met, tentatively at first; then, they were so engrossed with each other, they seemed to have forgotten about everyone else.

"Break it up," Aaron ran into the room. "Dad's coming for part two!"

Tapping on Troy's shoulder, he warned. "And he's got a shotgun."

Troy jolted away, sweating bullets. "Blame them, not me," he pointed at the crowd as he rubbed the back of his neck. Sheepish.

Her face as red as a ripe apple, Lydia laughed, the way she always did to cover her embarrassment. "Daddy's no murderer," she assured Troy. "At most, he'd shoot your leg to cripple you."

"Not a fan of that," Troy grumbled.

Uncle Denver, dressed as Santa Claus, strode into the hall. "Everyone, it's Birthday Cake time!"

Every year, Lydia's parents would dress up as Santa Claus and Mrs. Claus for Lydia's birthday party. This year was no exception. To her parents, Lydia was forever their baby girl.

A huge rose pink birthday cake awaited on a table decorated with white snowflakes, and pink unicorns at the center of the lawn.

It had on it the words,

"Happy Sweet Sixteenth Birthday, Lydia," iced in white.

Lydia and Troy lingered behind, making gooey eyes at each other, while the crowd gathered around the cake.

"We're missing something here," Uncle Denver announced.

"Lydia, Sweetie!" Aunt Sally ushered Lydia and Troy to the front of the group, right behind the center of the cake.

As they sang "Happy Birthday to Lydia," Abigail couldn't help but notice Troy holding Lydia's hand. Was it too soon to announce the pair as a new couple?

Troy helped Lydia cut and distribute the Birthday cake. Throughout the Christmas gift exchange, the newly-in-love couple hid behind the Christmas tree, lost in each other's eyes.

The party ended.

The guests bade their goodbyes.

Abigail checked on Lydia again, only to find her with Troy, oblivious to the rest of the world.

"Lydia," Abigail tapped her friend's shoulder.

The girl jumped. "Oh!"

"I've got to go now," said Abigail.

Lydia looked around, as if she'd just been awakened from a dream. "Where's everyone?"

"All gone home." Abigail left her friend in the arms of her new boyfriend. "Bye now, and Happy Birthday, Lydia!"

Four - Lydia : Orphaned

It was the Saturday before Christmas. Soft piped music filled the chambers. Chandeliers provided ambient light. Mouthwatering aromas surrounded them, yet the mood was sombre.

"I miss Daddy and Mummy," Lydia sighed, wiping away the wetness on her cheek with the back of her hand. It's unladylike, but who cares? She's with her brothers - not with anyone she had to impress.

"Me too," Ollie's hand covered her own.

"Same here," Aaron's hand clasped both his siblings'.

"Order whatever you want," Oliver handed her the menu. "It's our treat."

"Sorry I can't hang out with you on your birthday," Aaron caught her eye, a soft apology in his gaze. "Work commitments. I'm needed in Dubai to close the deal."

"I know," Lydia shrugged. "It's okay. We're celebrating my birthday and Christmas together now, aren't we?"

"Yeah," Ollie replied as he signalled the waiter to pop the champagne. "It's just a few days early. We're a call away."

"Your buddies are more important than me," Lydia pouted as she stared down Oliver, guilt-tripping her eldest brother.

"Hey," Oliver looked away. "This is the first time in a long while that Jayden, Ethan and Liam could free themselves from business commitments on Christmas Day."

"Yeah," Lydia sighed as the waiter filled their glasses. "I know how hard is for the four of you to meet these days."

"In memory of Dad and Mum," Oliver raised his glass.

"To Dad and Mum," Aaron and Lydia clinked their glasses with Ollie's

ON A BRIGHT AND CLEAR Christmas morning. Lydia was depressed. For the past few years, she would spend the Christmas holidays with Troy. This year's different: Troy left her for someone else a few months back.

The dulcet notes of the Christmas Carol, "Silent Night, Holy Night", played in the background, reminding her of Daddy and Mummy. They played it every Christmas, saying that's her song. It heralded her entry into this world.

Daddy would laugh, Mummy, giggle as they exchanged knowing looks at each other whenever the song played. Was her birth so silent. Did they sedate Mummy to take Lydia out of her womb?

Daddy and Mummy were so happy the last time she saw them. It was supposed to be a dream vacation in Africa.

They never returned.

Though they were proclaimed dead and a funeral was held in their memory, their bodies were never found.

Her vision blurred. She dried her eyes and stared at the Christmas tree, set up the way Daddy and Mummy always did. The big golden bell on top of the tree and little angels and colourful balls on its branches brought back fond childhood memories of a time long gone.

The phone rang.

"Hi, Lydia," Abigail's voice chirped. "Happy Birthday!"

"Thanks, Abby." The loneliness lifted. "And Merry Christmas to you."

"How's your day been so far?" Abigail asked.

"Okay, I guess," Lydia replied.

"Hey, I'm really sorry, but I can't make it today," said Abigail. "My boss called and wants me to work through Christmas to create a presentation for her to show her boss tomorrow."

"She can't do that!" Lydia hated how Abigail's boss bullied her.

"I told her I had something on. But she threatened to fire me if I didn't work on it today *and* send her hourly updates," Abigail moaned.

"That rabid female dog," Lydia sputtered.

"It's her designation. MAD," Abigail replied. "Gotta go now." She hung up.

Growing up, she found her brothers annoying.

Now she missed their company.

"Enough self pity," she chided herself. She grabbed the remote and turned on the television. There should be good Christmas programmes to keep her mind from spiralling.

The doorbell rang.

Who could it be?

A man carrying a cardboard box stood at her door.

She secured the chain and cracked the door open just enough to talk through the slit.

"Who is that?"

"This is for the family of Denver and Sally," the guy left the box at the doorstep and turned to walk away. The Beast Corp logo adorned the back of his jacket.

"Wait," she flung the door wide open. "Do you know what happened to Daddy and Mummy?"

The guy turned back.

Yellowed teeth showed through his grin.

"You must be Denver's daughter, Lydia." His eyes trailed from her face to her legs. Lydia shuddered. "We found their bodies and cremated them. Here are their ashes."

Lydia's stomach turned over.

The man extracted from the cardboard box an object that looked like a jewelry casket.

"The bodies of all the victims were mangled together," he handed her a gilded box. "The corpses were half-burnt, so we finished the job. Now we have to distribute the ashes to their families so that you can do whatever death rites you want."

"What?" Lydia's hands shook so hard, she almost dropped the keepsake urn. Trembling, she leaned against the wall for support.

"That's done. I'll recycle this." he picked up the empty cardboard box and walked away.

Her legs wobbled uncontrollably, forcing her to slide down the wall until she collapsed onto the floor. Hugging the ashes of her parents, she wept.

Lydia. It's your Daddy.

The voice came from the glowing, gilded box.

Five - Lydia : Bittersweet Reunion

"Joy to the world, the Lord is come!" Carollers sang in four part harmony while streaming into Denver's house.

Lydia's Daddy, once believed to be dead, had been alive all along[1]. That Daddy's-ashes-in-box thing had been a sham, all along.

Lydia snuggled under her Daddy's arm as they watched the performance. When she was little, she loved climbing onto his lap. She's too big for that now, so this was the best alternative.

Oliver, ever the eager host, brought out a tray of drinks for their thirsty guests. Traces of confetti clung to the hair of the carollers, even as they put on angelic expressions and sang Christmas hymns.

It seemed like yesterday when Lydia, Aaron and Oliver went from house to house with the other Sunday School kids, singing Christmas carols.

Her heart clenched at the memories of her brother, Aaron. They squabbled a lot back then. Born one year apart, people treated them like twins. Aaron and Lydia did everything together. At times, she even hated Aaron.

Now, he's dead. Killed by that reckless driver[2]. Her heart yearned for her brother.

Her vision blurred.

Blinking away the tears, she put on a smile. This was supposed to be a joyous occasion. She didn't want to rain on the parade.

"I'm here," Daddy pulled her close, as if he could read her mind. "I miss him too, but we'll meet again in heaven."

As the singers performed the hymn "Angels We Have Heard On High," she found her self singing the alto part, which she used to perform as a caroller, a long time ago.

The performance was as she remembered it. It was strange watching the carollers as a member of the audience.

She made sure they had roast turkey, roast beef and pizza waiting for the little singers. That was what she looked forward to the most, during her carolling days.

When the carollers finished their performance, she invited them to help themselves to the food and drinks she had prepared. The delight on their faces was worth all the time and money spent preparing the feast for these precious kids.

"No! I spilled grape juice on my new dress," a young girl tugged her white dress in despair.

Lydia had that covered.

She brought out the portable stain remover she kept handy for such situations.

"This will remove all the juice," she said, as she applied the wipe to the stain on the distraught girl's skirt. "Your Mummy would never know," she whispered, conspiratorially.

"Thank you, Auntie Lydia," the little girl chirped.

Lydia was only twenty-six. Being addressed as "Auntie" made her feel ancient.

The hour was up. The carollers sang "We Wish You A Merry Christmas," as they walked into their formation, ending with "Merry Christmas! And Happy Birthday Auntie Lydia!"

"They knew?" She stared at Oliver.

"You told them." It seemed like the sort of thing he'd do.

Oliver winked back at her. "Happy Birthday, Sis."

The carollers sang "Feliz Navidad," as they streamed out of the house. They had another house to visit.

That night, Daddy and Oliver decided to hang out with Lydia, spending the night in Denver's house instead of going to church for the Candlelight Service. They wanted private family time, after all that had happened in the recent months.

"I wish I had come back sooner," Daddy lamented. "If only I had a chance to see Aaron before he was taken from us."

"You didn't have a choice," Ollie reminded Daddy. "If only I investigated your disappearance earlier. I should have suspected something was off."

"What's done is done," Lydia reminded the men in her life. "The important thing is Daddy is alive and here with us." She nuzzled against her dear old Daddy.

"What's more important is where you're going after all this," Daddy replied. Lydia tensed in anticipation of the preaching that would follow.

"Can we not talk about it right now?" Lydia straightened her back, putting some distance between her father and herself.

"Dad's right," Oliver leaned towards her. "We are living in the Last Days. Any time now, Jesus could come and rapture the Church."

Lydia felt claustrophobic, sandwiched between the two religious zealots.

"Give me a break," she groaned. "It's my birthday."

"You were born twenty-six years ago in the flesh," Daddy replied. "But are you born again?"

He quoted his favourite verse from the King James Bible, John 3:3.

"Jesus answered and said unto him, Verily, verily, I say unto thee, Except a man be born again, he cannot see the kingdom of God."

Lydia buried her throbbing head in her hands. "Please, not now."

That traitor, Oliver, sided Daddy. "Lydia, listen to us. There isn't much time. Do you have a personal relationship with Jesus?"

"Look, you two," her temper rising, Lydia replied. "I went to Sunday School every week and carolling every Christmas until adulthood. I go to church with you guys every Easter Sunday."

"That's playing church," Oliver replied. "Have you accepted Jesus Christ as your Lord and Saviour?"

"I know Jesus!" Lydia retorted. "I do Christian meditation and Christian yoga every morning. I chant his name to empty my mind and play Christian music in the background every morning while I do my yoga stretches."

Denver rubbed his temple.

Oliver face palmed.

"Lydia, chanting a word to empty your mind is an occult practice that opens you up to demonic attacks. Yoga is the physical aspect of Hinduism and playing Christian music in the background does not change that fact," Oliver explained.

"You have your truth, I have mine. I am one with the Universe — the force that is God," Lydia replied.

"Lydia, sweetie, God created the Universe. The creator is not the creation," Denver took her hand.

"Jesus is God born as a human baby boy, who grew up fully God and fully man. He lived a sinless life here on earth, which qualified him to be the perfect once and for all sacrifice for ALL the sins of EVERYONE in the world. Then he died on the cross to pay for all sins."

Oliver took her other hand and quoted Romans 10:9-10 from the King James Bible.

"That if thou shalt confess with thy mouth the Lord Jesus, and shalt believe in thine heart that God hath raised him from the dead, thou shalt be saved.

For with the heart man believeth unto righteousness; and with the mouth confession is made unto salvation."

It's two against one. Knowing she couldn't win this argument, Lydia replied, "Give me time. Let me think about, okay?"

"There is no time," Denver grabbed her arms. "Don't you see the signs around us? The war in the Middle East. The earthquakes. Hurricanes. Look at the signs in the sky!"

Daddy had gone into full nut job mode.

Lydia wriggled free and covered both her ears. "Enough! This is my birthday. Don't ruin it for me!"

The ground shook, throwing her off her feet.

Daddy reacted immediately.

"Drop, Cover and Hold on," he pushed Lydia under a heavy table, diving after her, forming a human shield against the chaos, bearing the brunt of any falling debris.

His face twisted in pain, as he bit back a painful cry.

"Daddy!" Lydia cried.

"It's nothing," Daddy smiled. "I've taken bigger hits," he gripped the table's legs as the table rocked and the ground trembled.

Metal clattered, glass shattered and objects crashed around the house. Her heart skipped a beat as she heard the structure of the house creak.

"It's okay, sweetie," Daddy whispered, comforting her. "It will pass. Hold on tight."

Another jolt.

Her grip slipped.

Daddy caught her, pushing her back in where she reached for and clung to the table legs again. She couldn't stop shaking.

"Shh, little Lydia," Daddy held her close, singing her childhood lullaby, cocooning her in her father's love, calming Lydia's frazzled nerves.

The tremors finally stopped.

"Are you guys okay?" Oliver called.

"Lydia's hurt," Daddy helped Lydia out from under the table.

Oliver took one look at Lydia's forehead. "You're bleeding. I'll get first aid."

"Daddy, your shoulder." Her father's bloodied shirt worried her.

"It's nothing, " he chuckled. "I had worse. I'm more worried about you."

She touched the painful wetness on her head with her finger. It came away bloodied. "Oh this," she said. "Doesn't hurt much."

"You still need to get it disinfected," Daddy advised while Oliver returned with the first aid kit.

"Yes, Daddy," Lydia chuckled.

"What I'm more worried about is, are you ready to meet the Lord?" Daddy refused to let the subject go.

"Daddy!" Lydia pouted.

Daddy sighed. "Plan B it is then."

That piqued Lydia's curiosity. "What Plan B?"

"If anything happens to your brother and me, you must go with Leo," Daddy said, his voice laden with gravity. "He owes me. He'll come for you and take you to a safe place."

Six - Lydia : Leo

"**H**appy Birthday, Lydia!" Daddy and Oliver showed up on Christmas morning at Lydia's apartment. She decided to move out of the family home to get away from Daddy's constant preaching.

Oliver held the strings of a massive bunch of pink and white balloons that floated just above his head. Daddy carried a box from her favourite cake shop.

"Daddy! Ollie!" Lydia hugged the two men in her life.

"I thought you had a party on Jayden's yacht today," Lydia stared at her eldest brother.

"Tend to the most important things first," Oliver laughed. "Baby sister's birthday first. Christmas party later. I told the guys I'll be late."

"C'mon sweetie," Daddy ruffled her hair. "Let's do the cake!"

Oliver tied bunches of balloons to the furniture in her apartment while Daddy set up the birthday cake.

Lydia watched tiny flames dance on two large candles and seven small ones - mesmerised.

Happy Birthday to you.
Happy Birthday to you.
Happy Birthday to Lydia.
Happy Birthday to you.

Daddy and Oliver sang in perfect two part harmony, with Oliver singing tenor while Daddy singing bass.

Feeling like a little girl once more, Lydia blew out the flames with one big puff while Ollie took a selfie group photo with his old polaroid camera. Sometimes, the old ways are best.

He held the photograph as the trio watched the photograph develop in front of their eyes.

"Your missing loved ones are alive and well in the care of our Alien benefactors," the charismatic man announced. "Their ridiculous beliefs held back our collective evolution. Hence our Alien benefactors removed them, so that we who are left behind, may advance."

That story had been repeated to the entire world every day since the Rapture. A number of the world's key leaders had been raptured, leaving a power vacuum, which opportunists jumped in to fill.

"They have given me the technology to turn humans into superhuman," Beast continued. "If you would like to among the first to make that quantum leap in evolution, sign up at your nearest Beast Corp centre."

As he spoke, fiery hail fell from the sky, destroying the stage and all the newly transplanted grass and trees around it.

The dorm door slid open.

A gorgeous man in his late twenties walked in with a covered tray.

"Merry Christmas, Ladies," a deep baritone accompanied his brilliant smile.

Tess froze.

Starstruck.

That girl had a humongous crush on Jayden, one of the Ark's founders and Leo's righthand man.

"May I?" His eyes twinkled as he entered the conversation pit and laid the tray on the table.

The heartthrob removed the cover to reveal three servings of turkey and potatoes with three glasses of cranberry juice. "Enjoy!"

The heavenly aroma made Lydia's mouth water. She tucked in.

"Aren't you eating with us?" Tess batted her eyelashes at her crush, as she picked at her food - too smitten to eat.

"No," he flashed his signature smile. "I will be eating with the guys after we've distributed Christmas lunch to everyone."

With his arms crossed and a nonchalant air, he leaned against the wall, looking every bit a male model that would make teenage girls' hearts flutter.

The siren went off.

"Evacuation drill," he smirked. Of course Jayden knew. He's The Ark's head of operations.

"Move! You have fifteen minutes to get to the Emergency Assembly Area." He started his timer.

Lydia swallowed the last of her turkey and dashed for the vent. She knew the route like the back of her hand, having gone through it countless times.

Scrambling on her knees and hands, Lydia followed behind Betty, through the maze of tunnels.

"You have five minutes," she could hear Jayden's voice in the distance.

"Hurry," She nudged Betty.

"I'm hurrying. I'm hurrying," Betty muttered as she crawled at a speedier pace.

"Fourteen minutes and thirty-six seconds," Jayden announced as Tess, the last of the group, dropped out of the tunnel. How he got the ahead of them was anyone's guess. He probably had a secret, shorter route.

Out in the open, they had to lie low to avoid unwanted attention.

It has been a year since her last Christmas with her family. Though she missed them, she was happy on their behalf.

They escaped God's wrath.

The ground was razed from fiery hail. Many farms had been destroyed. The Ark's founders had the foresight to set up underground farms that provided the occupants with just enough food to stave off hunger.

From a distance, she heard "Last Christmas" performed.

Peeking through the bushes, she watched how Christmas was celebrated in this dystopian new world:

Beneath the large "Merry Xmas" banner, scantily clad people of indeterminate gender partied in drunken revelry around Christmas trees — in this Christ-less Christmas.

The only difference between the scene before her and some of the more "liberal" parties she witnessed was this:

The central figure that anchored the Xmas holiday, Santa Claus, wore Beast's face.

Eight - Lydia : Red Christmas

"I'm dreaming of a white Christmas," or so the famous Christmas song goes. This year, it wasn't a white Christmas, but a red one — blood red.

God is real.

She shuddered as she witnessed His wrath unleashed on those who rejected Him.

God is merciful.

Since the day she surrendered to Jesus, giving up her old crutches - her crystals, yoga, meditation practices to empty the mind, and all the new age practices she once cherished, she found a peace in spite of the chaos around her.

It took the shock of being left behind when Jesus came for his Bride to wake her up.

It's her birthday. She used to celebrate the mornings with her family and Christmas after that. With her entire family in heaven, she decided to celebrate her birthday with me-time by the beach.

She may be living in an underground bunker, but she wasn't a prisoner there. "Lydia to Central Control," she tapped her Leotech earbud. "It's my birthday today. I am going to the beach via route A and will be back in four hours."

"Noted," Selena, who was on duty that day, replied.

The Ark's motto was "leave none of our brethren behind."

Jezebel and the entire harlot church actively hunted down known and suspected Bible believers for reprogramming or slaughter. Anyone who had been in close contact with the raptured, or who had attended church in the past, were on the suspect list. By that definition, every one in The Ark was on Jezebel's hit list.

It was the fear of persecution that kept residents from the leaving The Ark, unless they had important business outside. Lydia knew that some of the guys

Nine - Lydia : 200,000,000

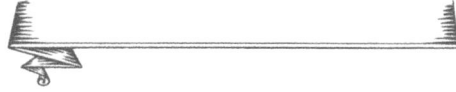

"Wake up!"

Someone turned on the lights and pulled the blankets off Lydia.

Although there's no sunrise or sunset underground, bright lights mimicking daylight, lit the Ark's common areas during daylight hours — while dim light, mimicking the moon and stars, lit the neighbourhood after that. According to Lydia's body clock it wasn't even five, that Christmas morning.

"Mmph," Lydia wrestled back the blanket and rolled herself in it.

Selena yanked it away. "Get up, sleepy head. All hands on deck for an emergency search and rescue."

Lydia jolted awake as Selena handed her a Scorched Earth Camouflage bodysuit.

"Conference room in ten minutes," Selena barked as she left the room.

Leo conducted the briefing. The screen behind him displayed photographs of five men and two women - new believers they were to rescue and shelter, if they were still alive.

An army of two hundred thousand, thousand horsemen were sweeping through the land, killing indiscriminately. Their intel team received a call for help from a cluster of new believers there.

Ethan, Lydia and Selena were assigned to retrieve Chloe from the war zone. Ethan's device locked onto Chloe's co-ordinates.

The putrid stench of smoke, sulphur, blood and death welcomed the trio when they stepped out of their transport.

From her hiding place in the alley, the horses looked terrifying. Each had breastplates of fire, jacinth and brimstone. The horses had lions heads that breathed out fire, smoke and brimstone. If that wasn't bad enough, they had serpents for tails.

"Do not engage," Ethan whispered. "Wait for the army to pass before we search for her."

If Lydia had a superpower, it would be invisibility. Growing up, no one noticed her in a crowded room. In the battlefield, that's a boon.

Hiding in the shadows of the alley, Lydia thought her racing heart would give her away.

Steeling herself, she would not let terror consume her.

"Lord, give me strength and courage to do this," she prayed in silence.

The last of the horses galloped away.

Silence fell.

Burning Christmas trees lit the terrain.

The charred remains of Santa Beast lay in the middle of the town square.

"Over there," Evan pointed at a group of men attacking a lone woman. You would think that after such shared horror, people would band together to help the injured. Instead, what unfolded was a disgusting scene of opportunists taking advantage of those who can't defend themselves.

After stealing her belongings, the men were stripping away her dignity.

Lydia's blood boiled with rage. She wanted to tear them apart for their atrocities.

"Now," Ethan whispered, anger burning in his eyes.

The trio charged as one, breaking up the mob.

Lydia kicked the arm that held Chloe, forcing the hoodlum to release his grip. Selena finished the job with a roundhouse kick, knocking the guy out.

Ethan punched out one guys.

Lydia kicked another unconscious.

The rest of the assailants fled.

WITH A GENTLE SMILE, Ethan bent over and carried the injured woman, bridal style.

"This is Chloe," he introduced her like an old friend. "Her brother helped me grow crops to feed us, so she gets a place in The Ark."

"It's been two years already," Lydia frowned. "Why didn't she join us sooner?"

"I had no idea it would get this bad," Chloe's voice was a harsh whisper. Blood trickled down the back of her head. She could be concussed. They had to keep her awake until the medics could see to her.

From Selena's rapid typing on her communicator, she must have noticed it too.

"She stayed on her own. Her brother was raptured. We assumed she was too," Ethan said. "It was a miracle we found her."

Chloe's eyelids drooped.

Lydia addressed Chloe so that she wouldn't fall asleep.

"Why did they think you were raptured?"

"People tend to assume that since I served in church and don't swear, I had to be saved," Chloe shrugged as Ethan carried her into the vehicle. "No one told me you had to be born again[3] and have a relationship with Jesus to be saved."

"Oh," Lydia was speechless. Chloe was left behind because she was clueless. Lydia knew better but was a stubborn fool.

"How did you survive?" Lydia asked.

"God's providence," Chloe mumbled.

They reached The Ark's medical facility.

While Ethan carried her in, Lydia kept up the conversation.

"What did you do?" Lydia asked.

"In these past two years?" Chloe picked at her ragged fingernails. "I've been running for my life from Jezebel's hoodlums, hiding from falling balls of fire, looking for drinkable water, selling everything I had for food. Then I got stung by demonic locusts with human faces and scorpion stings."

Lydia shuddered at the memory of those tormentors that sprung from the ground and attacked everyone in The Ark. No one died but everyone suffered for five months.

"It's by God's grace that I'm still alive," she whispered as the medic took over.

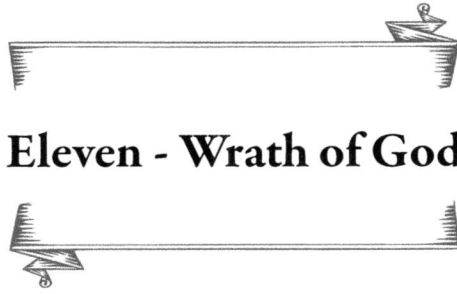

Eleven - Wrath of God

The Ark was in full lockdown mode: Birthday or not, no one was to leave their assigned dorms.

Leo kept the Holy Bible with him. This was how he predicted the events in the outside world. It was the time of the bowl or vial judgements, where God would pour his wrath on the earth.

Thanks to Liam's generous funding, every dorm had screens portraying world events, recorded by Leo's nano-spy cam drones all over the world. In Lydia's dorm, the primary focus was in Beast's throne room where multitudes of sycophants worshipped him.

How Leo got his nano-bots undetected within the heart of the dictator's abode baffled Lydia, but she wasn't complaining. That's where most of the action would take place.

"It came upon a midnight clear, that glorious, song of old." The dulcet notes of the old Christmas hymn streamed from the CD player perched on Lydia's closet.

Lydia, Ava, Tess and Chloe huddled together, watching the terrifying scenes unfold, through The Ark's television network. It was worse than any horror movie.

It was real.

The sky darkened.

A man in a business suit— immaculately groomed — headed towards a skyscraper.

He had the mark of the beast in his forehead.

You had to have the mark of the beast to hold any form of employment these days.

As he walked towards the office building, blisters erupted covering his skin, growing in size; some filling with pus, others turning into open ulcers, as the man let out an agonising scream..

A woman pushing a trolley of groceries past him, cried.

Horrified.

Lesions broke out all over her flawless skin.

Cowering in pain, she covered her face.

She had Beast's mark in her right hand.

All over the world, men and women who had taken the mark of the beast screamed as grievous sores erupted all over their bodies.

Impoverished outcasts—in dirty rags—who slept on the sidewalks because they couldn't earn a living and had no means to afford a roof over their heads, were unaffected by the sudden plague.

It only affected those who had taken Beast's mark.

Lydia's stomach turned over at the gruesome sight.

"And so it begins," Selena grimaced with her eyes fixated on the screen.

"Look," Betty gawked at the sea-facing screens.

An angel—too dazzling to behold— emerged from the sky carrying a vial filled with power. Deliberately, he emptied it into the sea, triggering a violent reaction from the water, causing it to boil and thicken into a crimson viscous liquid, comparable to the blood of a dead man.

Fish leaped out of the water.

Vibrant corals turned ghostly.

As the surface of the sea was covered with the underbellies of dead marine life, the ocean emitted a deadly vapour, suffocating all living beings on it, killing every living soul out at sea.

"It's not just the ocean," Chloe gestured at the telecast of events happening in parks. The bubbling brooks and gushing fountains turned into blood, to the horrified, collective gasps of onlookers.

"All the water sources that have turned into blood."

"Are we affected?" Feeling sickened by what she had witnessed, Lydia asked Selena.

"The Ark's founders knew this would happen, so they stocked up bottled water to last us until The Lord returns," Selena replied.

On another screen, the dark skies brightened. The sun pierced through the smog — its light, blinding.

Those who were caught outdoors turned as red as lobsters, blisters forming on their sunburnt skin, as the sun's relentless heat scorched them.

"That's why Leo insisted everyone stays in the dorms," Betty murmured, her eyes fixed on the screen.

Blinding light faded as darkness consumed Beast's kingdom. Hideous screams emerged from the inhabitants there. From within the throne room, Beast roared with fury and agony.

"Why don't they repent?" Betty frowned. "All that should wake them up."

Instead, the girls heard defiant curses, directed at God in Heaven.

"It's coming to a a close," Selena gestured at the scene of the great river Euphrates, now dried up. The caked ground prepared the way for the kings of the east to march through.

The amazonian woman stooped to enter the room. Her presence filled the entire space. "Take the mark of the beast and receive power and riches untold," she crooned. "Reject Beast and die."

Taking Beast's mark meant pledging allegiance to the devil and turning her back on her Lord and Saviour.

Lydia straightened her posture, holding her head high with an arrogant air. She took her time to turn and face the invader.

"What power and riches can he offer?" She quirked an eyebrow as she faced the blonde.

"Whatever you want, you will get," Emma's laughter tinkled. "Beauty. Perfection. Strength."

"How is that possible?" Lydia tilted her head, feigning interest, to delay Emma.

"Beast will give you a new body - one far better than the pathetic form you currently inhabit," Emma locked eyes with her.

Tess and Chloe should have enough of a head start by now.

"No," She replied. Supernatural courage filled her, God's love overflowing her heart. "I choose Jesus. I reject the mark of the beast."

"Then die."

Flames engulfed Emma's hand.

With a wicked smirk, Beast's warrior incinerated Lydia.

The very instant that Lydia's physical body was destroyed, the Lord's power enveloped her spirit and soul. Jesus Christ, the real meaning of Christmas, received her in heaven. Her heart overflowed with love.

She took his outstretched hand and followed The Lord to the throne of God Himself. There, she was bestowed a white robe and granted an honoured place to rest and wait under the altar of the Holy God.

Revelation 7:14-17 KJV

And I said unto him, Sir, thou knowest. And he said to me, These are they which came out of great tribulation, and have washed their robes, and made them white in the blood of the Lamb.

Therefore are they before the throne of God, and serve him day and night in his temple: and he that sitteth on the throne shall dwell among them.

They shall hunger no more, neither thirst any more; neither shall the sun light on them, nor any heat.

For the Lamb which is in the midst of the throne shall feed them, and shall lead them unto living fountains of waters: and God shall wipe away all tears from their eyes.

---

[1] See Emunah Short Stories Book 2: Oliver and Emunah Short Stories Book 3: Emunah.

[2] See Emunah Short Stories Book 1: Abigail.

[3] KJV

John 1:12-13

But as many as received him, to them gave he power to become the sons of God, even to them that believe on his name: Which were born, not of blood, nor of the will of the flesh, nor of the will of man, but of God.

John 3:3-7 Jesus answered and said unto him, Verily, verily, I say unto thee, Except a man be born again, he cannot see the kingdom of God. Nicodemus saith unto him, How can a man be born when he is old? can he enter the second time into his mother's womb, and be born? Jesus answered, Verily, verily, I say unto thee, Except a man be born of water and of the Spirit, he cannot enter into the kingdom of God. That which is born of the flesh is flesh; and that which is born of the Spirit is spirit. Marvel not that I said unto thee, Ye must be born again.

1 Peter 1:23 Being born again, not of corruptible seed, but of incorruptible, by the word of God, which liveth and abideth for ever.

Romans 10:9 That if thou shalt confess with thy mouth the Lord Jesus, and shalt believe in thine heart that God hath raised him from the dead, thou shalt be saved.

[4] For their love story, read The Quest for Immortality, by Janice Wee.

Don't miss out!

Visit the website below and you can sign up to receive emails whenever Janice Wee publishes a new book. There's no charge and no obligation.

https://books2read.com/r/B-A-BTWW-WVYGF

BOOKS 2 READ

Connecting independent readers to independent writers.

Max the Cat
The Scouts
Escape To Long Hill
Max & Friends

Tales From Singapore
Singapore's Runaway
Two Worlds, One Love & a Serial Killer
Two Worlds
Naughty Little Nonya
Little Nonya's Escapades

Standalone
Escape
Sweetcorn Suzie

Watch for more at www.janicewee.com.

About the Author

Janice Wee is Straits Born Chinese from Singapore.

She is a sixth generation Singaporean, the daughter of two English teachers and who spent her childhood in libraries.

Learn more about the worlds and characters in her stories in her website janicewee.com

Read more at www.janicewee.com.

9 798230 251316